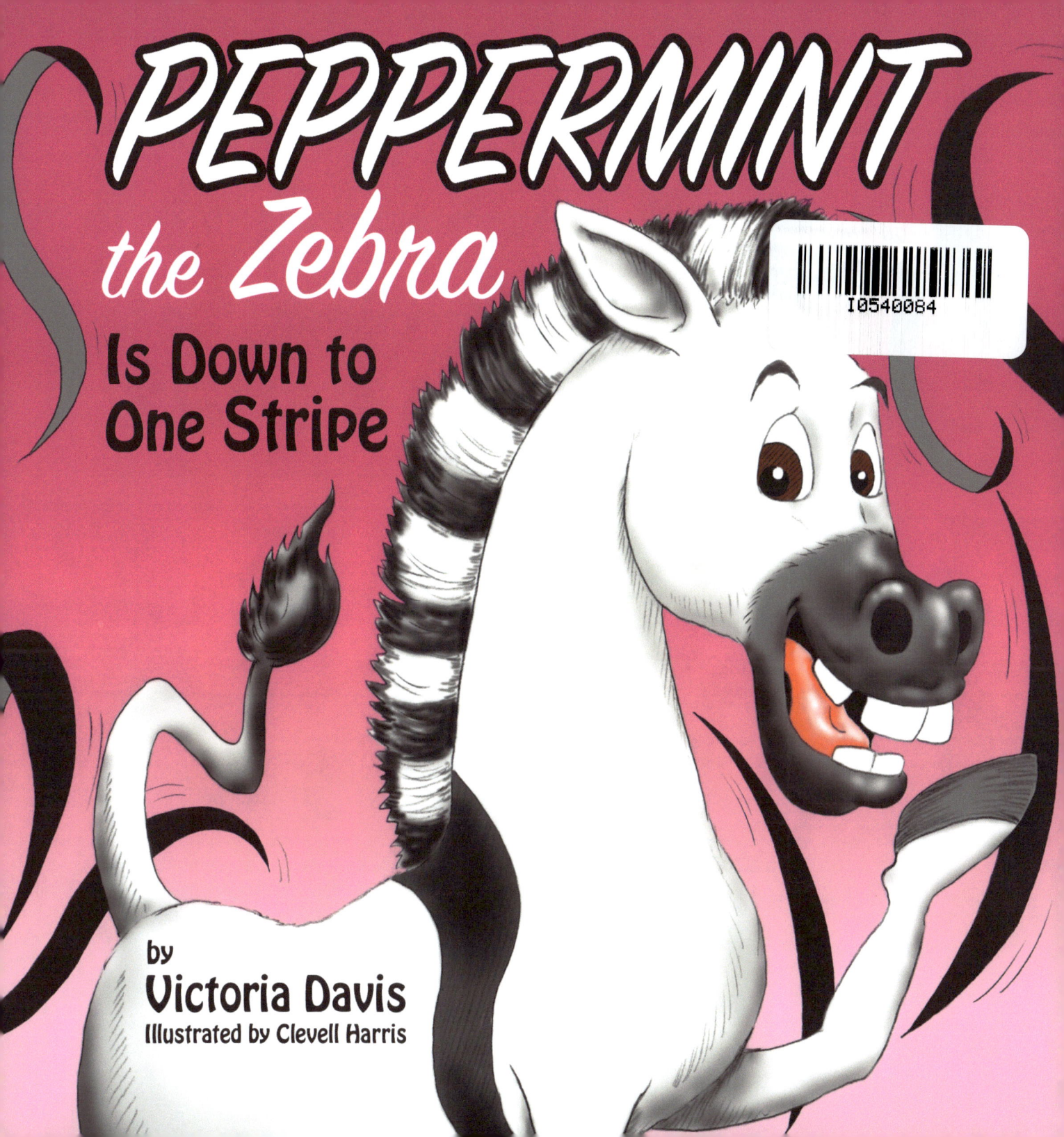

PEPPERMINT
the Zebra
Is Down to One Stripe

by
Victoria Davis
Illustrated by Clevell Harris

How did Peppermint the Zebra lose his stripes?

Did he **sneeze**, did he **cough**, did he **growl** all night?

No no no... that's just not right!

That's not how Peppermint got down to one stripe!

How did Peppermint the Zebra lose his stripes?

Did he run really fast or JUMP really high?

Did he roll on his belly to stomp his stripes out?

Go! Peppermint Go!

No no no... that's just not right!

That's not how Peppermint got down to one stripe!

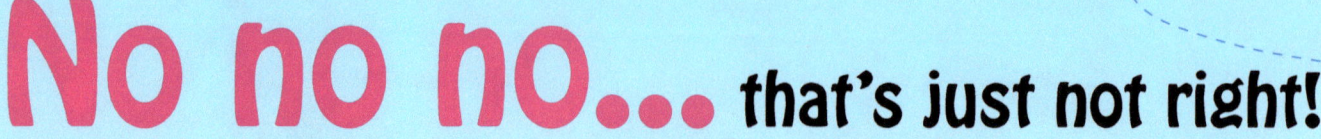

1,2,3,4,5..

How did Peppermint the Zebra lose his stripes?

Did he flap his tail or **wiggle** his ears?

Did he close his eyes and count to ten?

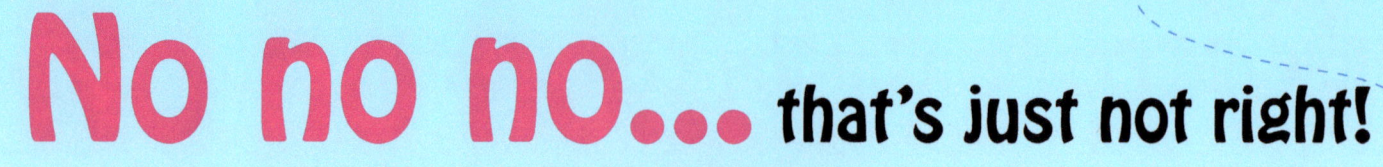
No no no... that's just not right!

That's
not how
Peppermint got
down to one
stripe!

How did Peppermint the Zebra lose his stripes?

Did he **tell** a friend and make a wish?

Did he dream so big that his stripes disappeared?

No no no... that's just not right!

That's not how Peppermint got down to one stripe!

How did Peppermint the Zebra lose his stripes?

Did he use bubbles or water to **wash** them all off? Did he yell really loudly in a zebra-like voice?

How did Peppermint the Zebra lose his Stripes?

Did he blow them away with a great big **kiss?**

Did he whistle to a song that made his cheeks twist?

No no no... that's just not right!

That's not how Peppermint got down to one stripe!

So...how did Peppermint the Zebra lose his stripes?

He gave them away one by one to share
with his friends who had none.

That's how Peppermint the Zebra got down to one stripe!

For my daughter, Victoria Elizabeth and my son,
Alphonso Fitzgerald... you are truly the best parts of me
and the greatest joy of my life.

With all my love, may your journey in learning and reading
continue and be everlasting! ~Mom

Special thanks to all my little reader's!

I'm so grateful for my journey,
~V. Davis

Do not neglect your gift, which was given to you.
~1 Timothy 4:14

For more information write to the Author, Victoria Davis

5300 N. Braeswood Blvd. Suite 346
Houston, Texas 77096
Or Email: vdavis9000@yahoo.com

Available to order on amazon

www.ingramcontent.com/pod-product-compliance
Lightning Source LLC
Chambersburg PA
CBHW041006170626
46815CB00002B/181